Whose Nose?

Written by Fiona Munro
Illustrated by John Haslam
Designed by Nicola Theobald

Ladybird

I hurry along with my nose to the ground.
I can smell something lovely.
Look what I've found!

Can you guess who I am
by my little pink snout?
I use it for sniffing
and snuffling about!

My trunk's just great
for keeping cool.
I love lounging around
by a muddy pool!

who am I with a nose so pink and tiny,
a long thin tail and eyes so shiny?

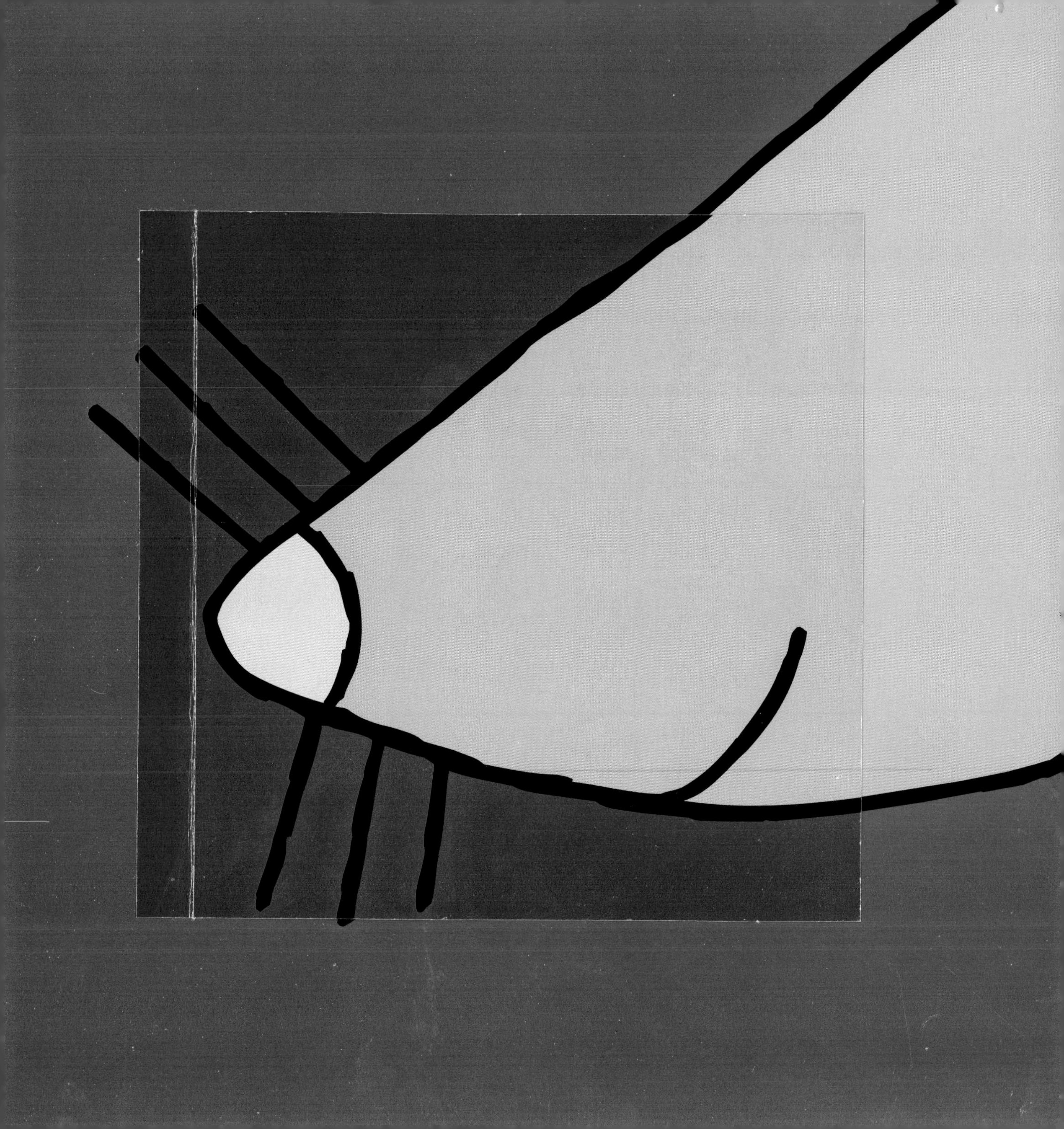

I've got a nose like a furry purry cat.
But I'm not quite as soft or cuddly as that!

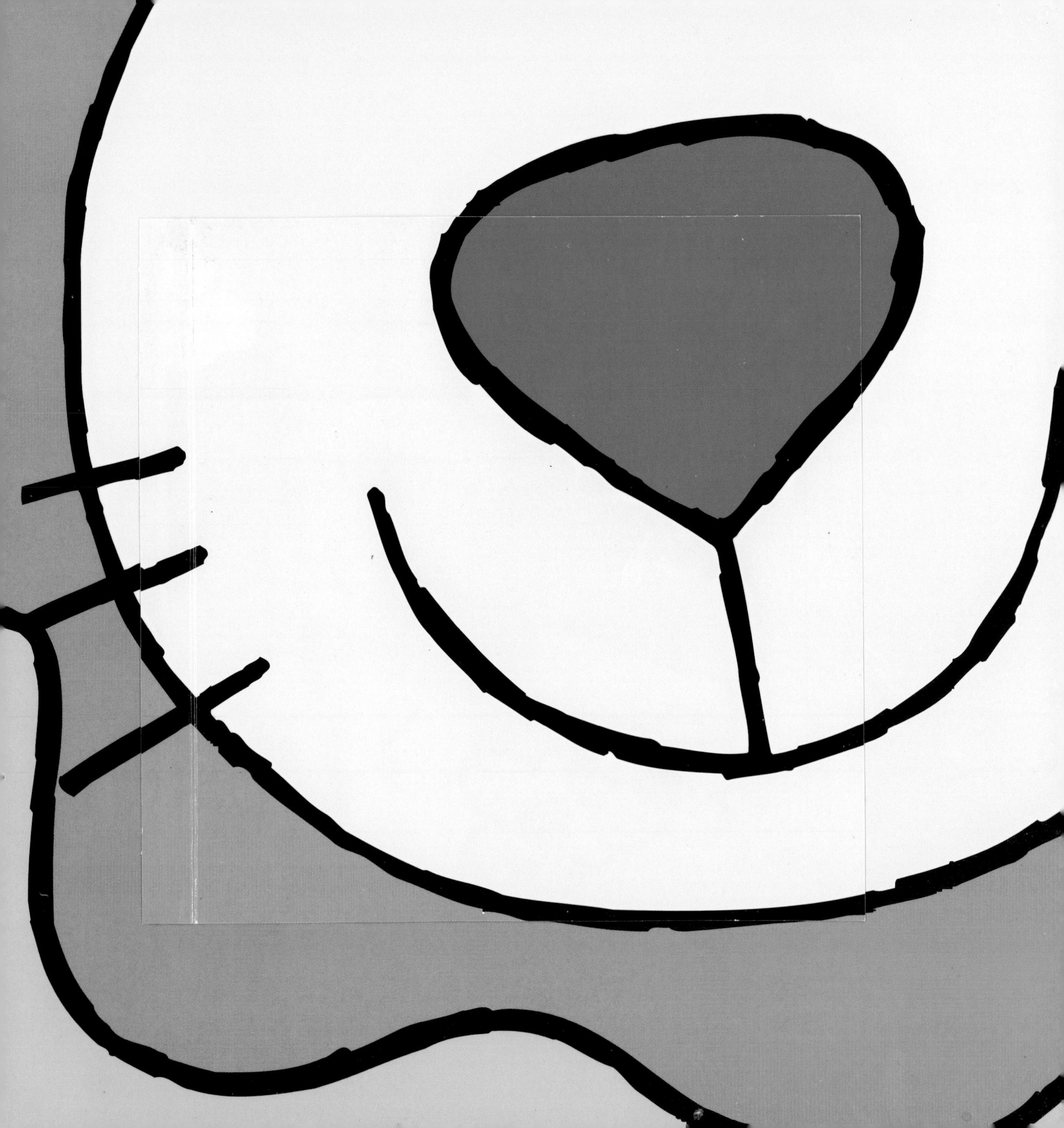

We snort and we sniffle and snuffle, too.
Wouldn't our noses
look silly on you?